Little Jashanafar

Hanukkah
Coloring and Activity Book

Count the items and connect them with a line to the correct answer.

3

6
2

Find 6 differences between the pictures.

Color them all !

for Kids

THIS BOOK BELONGS TO:

○○○○○○○○○○○○○○○○○○○○○○○○○○○

Dear customer.
Thank you for purchasing this book.
Your feedback means a lot to us,
as it allows our team to create
more and more interesting
and exceptional content.
Thank you again for your support.

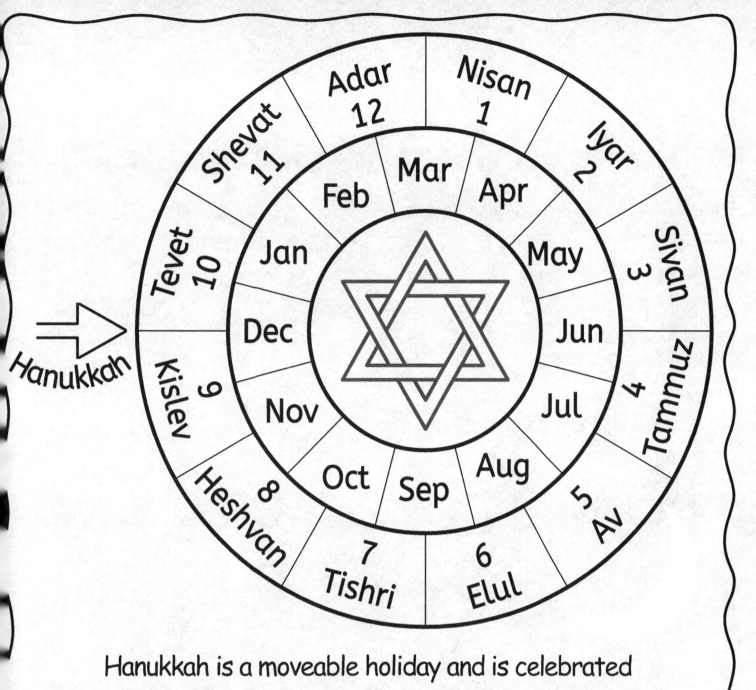

Hanukkah is a moveable holiday and is celebrated
on the 25th day of the month of Kislev and lasts
until the 2nd day of the month of Tevet
according to the Jewish calendar.
This holiday commemorates the miracle that happened
in the Jerusalem Temple.
The lit menorah, despite having enough oil for only one day
burned for as many as 8 days!
Therefore, we celebrate Hanukkah for 8 days.

TEST COLOR

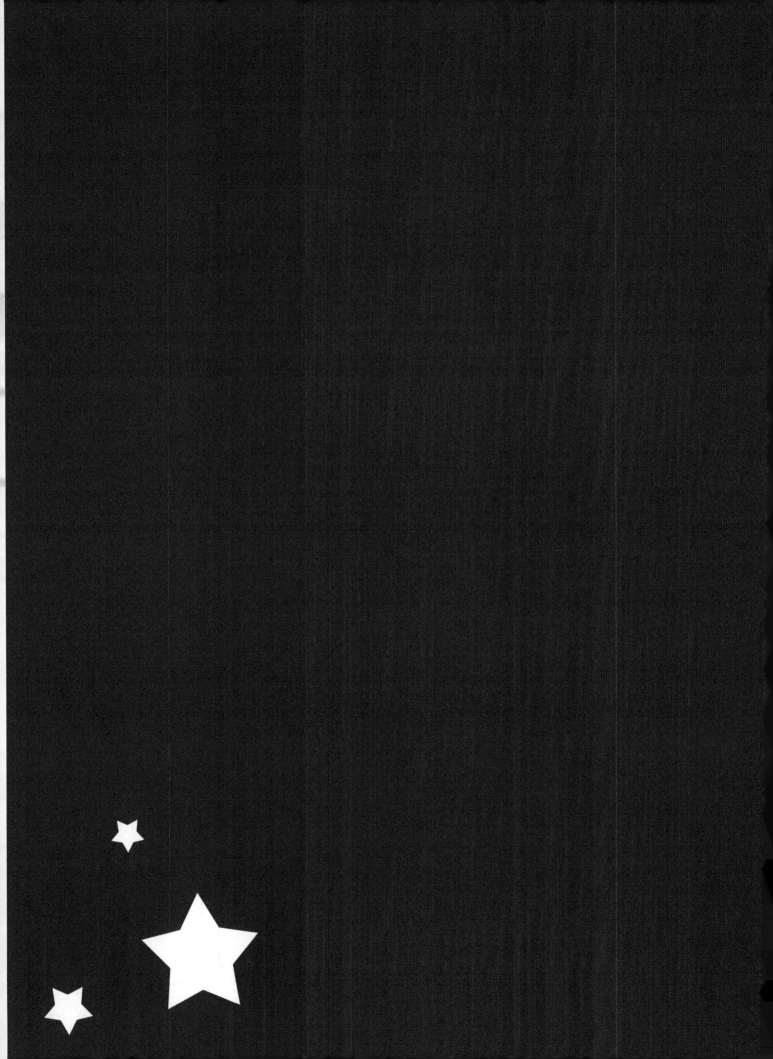

TEST COLOR

Find 8 words related to Hanukkah.
Search words in directions:

```
P D E D I C A T I O N M
C H A N U K A H L A T E
S I A T O R T H I N L N
W P A S S O V E R D E O
E B P L U T H C V L P R
E D R B E K O N S E R A
T C A R D S K A D L T H
S Q Y T E M P L E Q V S
A W I S H E S T A S E M
J U D A I S M I D H N S
N I G H M O O N T Y T E
W Q G Z F X A U A J C T
```

- moon
- passover
- Temple
- Judaism
- wishes
- sweets
- Tevet
- dedication

See the solution on the next page :)

```
P D E D I C A T I O N M
C F A J U K W H L A T E
S I A T O R T H I N L N
W P A S S O V E R D E O
E B R L U T H C V L P R
E D R B E K O N S E R A
T C D R D S K A D L T H
S Q Y T E M P L E Q V S
A W I S H E S T A S E M
J U D A I S M I D H N S
N I G H M O O N T Y T E
W Q G Z F X A U A J C T
```

The Hebrew letters on the dreidel are
the first letters of these words:

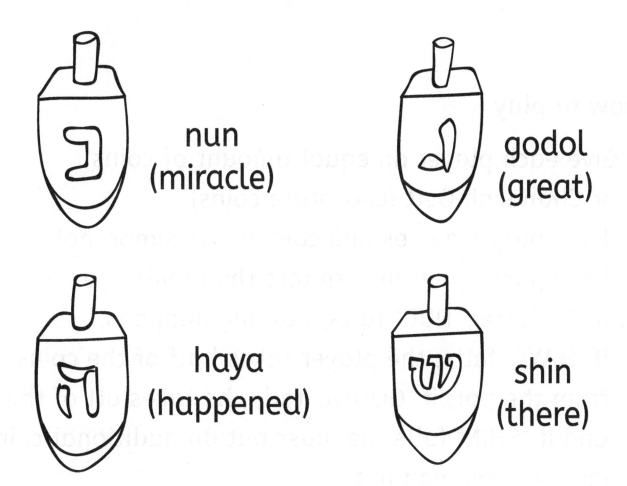

nun
(miracle)

godol
(great)

haya
(happened)

shin
(there)

Each letter symbolizes victory or defeat in the game,
and on the other side is the beginning of a word.
By spinning the dreidel, one randomly wins or loses
candy. At the same time, we put together
the sentence "a great miracle happened there"
(Hebrew: nes gadol haya sham).

How to play

1 Give each player an equal amount of coins
   or Chanukah Gelt (chocolate coins).
2. Each player places one coin in a common pot.
3. Each participant in turn lets the dreidel go.
4. If the letter "NUN" falls, nothing happens,
   if "HAYA" falls, the player takes half of the coins
   from the pot, if "GODOL" falls, he takes all of them,
   and if "SHIN" falls, he must put an additional coin
   into the common pot.
5. If a player runs out of gelt, he loses.
6. After each turn, players add one coin to the pot.
7. Play until one player wins all the coins.

Let's design your own Dreidel

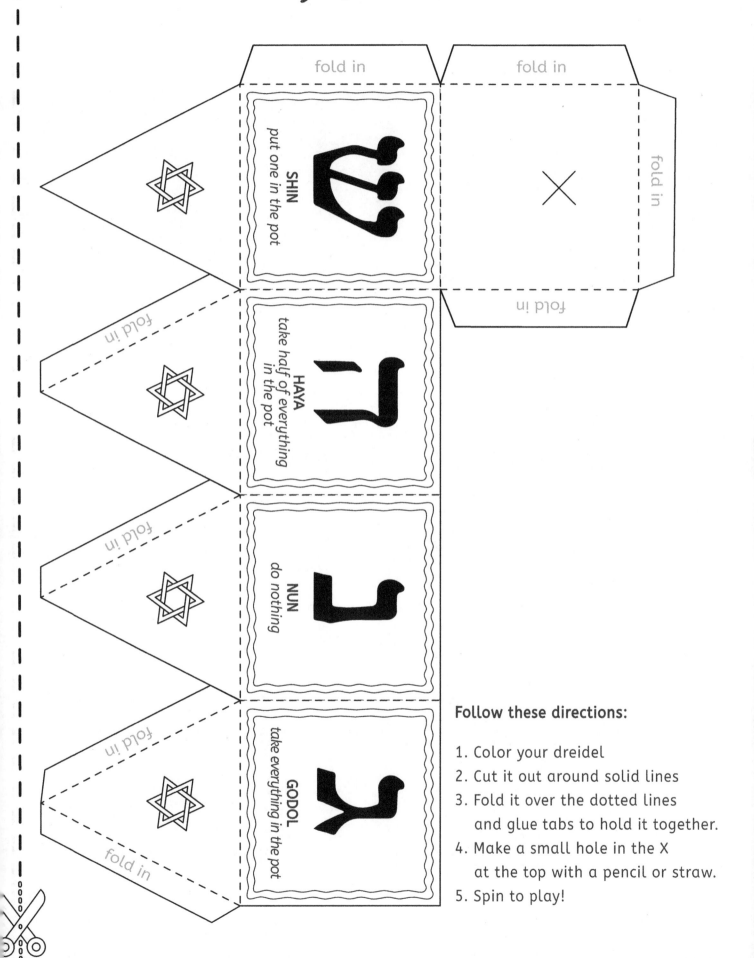

fold in fold in

fold in

×

SHIN
put one in the pot

fold in

HAYA
take half of everything
in the pot

fold in

fold in

NUN
do nothing

fold in

GODOL
take everything in the pot

fold in

Follow these directions:

1. Color your dreidel
2. Cut it out around solid lines
3. Fold it over the dotted lines
   and glue tabs to hold it together.
4. Make a small hole in the X
   at the top with a pencil or straw.
5. Spin to play!

Count the items and connect them with a line to the correct answer.

Color them all !

Find 6 differences between the pictures.

Color them all !

Connect the elements with their shadows with a line.

Color them all !

Hanukkah is celebrated
for eight days.

Help the flame find its way to candle :)
Good luck!

Learn how to draw a Hanukkiah! Draw a Hanukkiah according to the template below across the designated boxes

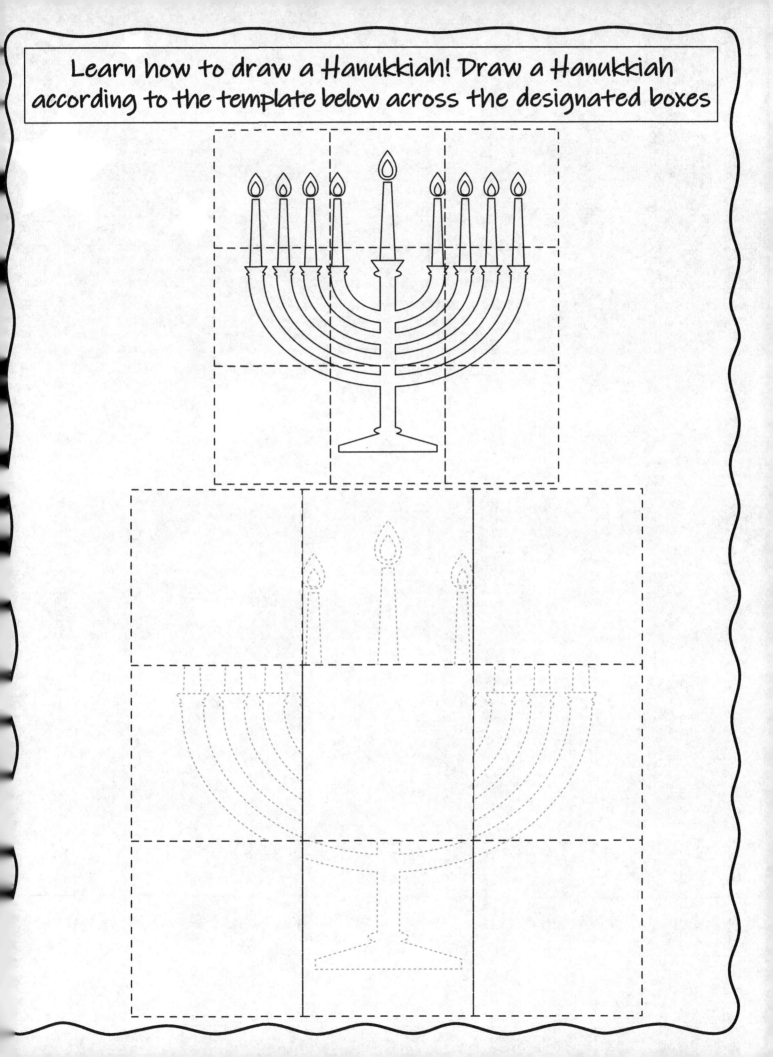

Find and pair with lines the same characters.

Color them all !

```
P E I G H T I O L N D R
H A N U K K A H C W T E
S E N I J B C H S I L F
T P M R V K A Q E N E L
A B T O R A H C D E H N
R C K B S R S W Z N R O
E M O U U M A A F L Y V
S C H I L D R E N I T E
A E Y O N D A T P S U M
T R J J A S W T B R L B
E S H T H N R I T Y I E
W S O G I F T G E O N R
```

- Hanukkah   - coins   - children
- star   - eight   - november
- gift   - torah

See the solution on the next page :)

```
P  E  I  G  H  T  I  O  L  N  D  R
H  A  N  U  K  K  A  H  C  W  T  E
S  E  N  I  J  B  C  H  S  I  L  F
T  P  M  R  V  K  A  Q  E  N  E  L
A  B  T  O  R  A  H  C  D  E  H  N
R  C  K  B  S  R  S  W  Z  N  R  O
E  M  O  U  U  M  A  A  F  L  Y  V
S  C  H  I  L  D  R  E  N  I  T  E
A  E  Y  O  N  D  A  T  P  S  U  M
T  R  J  J  A  S  W  T  B  R  L  B
E  S  H  T  H  N  R  I  T  Y  I  E
W  S  O  G  I  F  T  G  E  O  N  R
```

Count the items and connect them with a line to the correct answer.

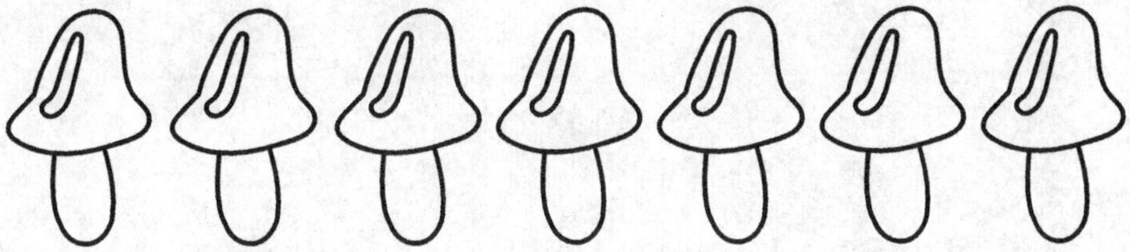

5

7

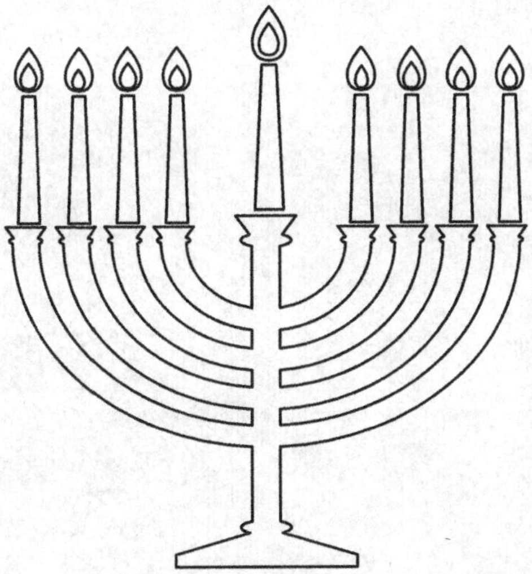

3

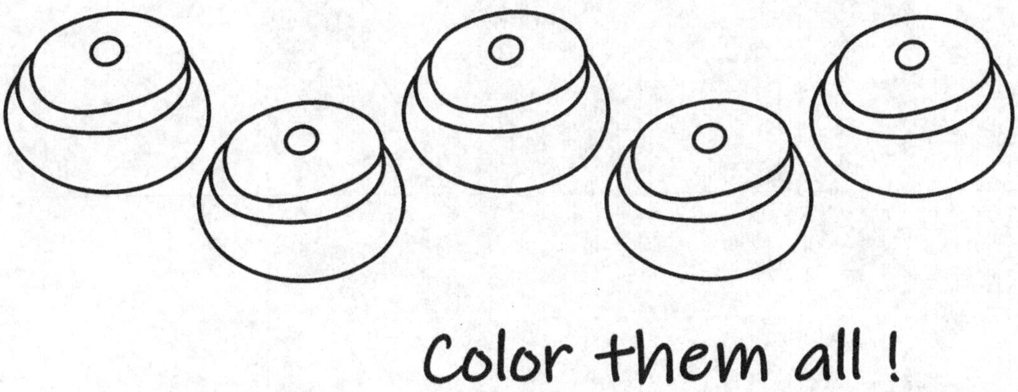

1

Color them all !

Write the missing letters in the blank
Spaces so that they form the correct word

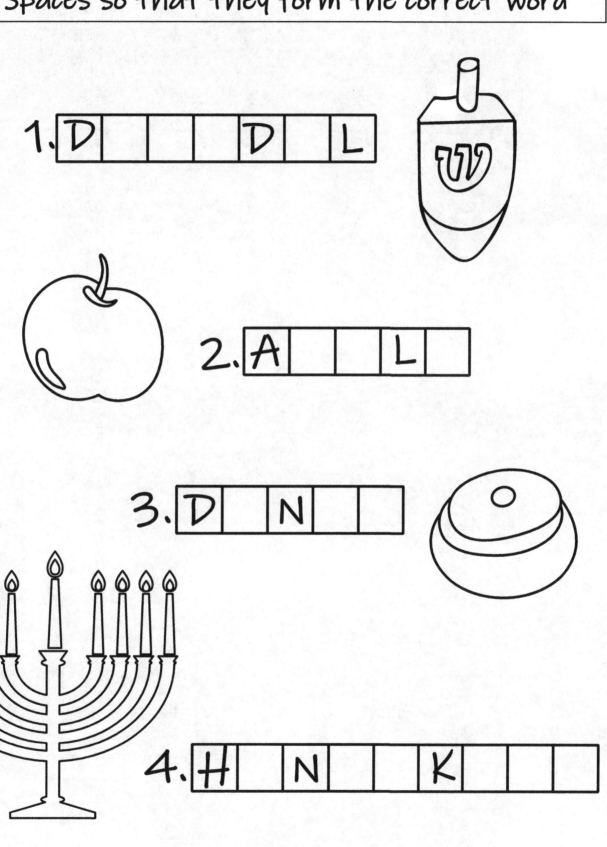

1. D □ □ □ D L

2. A □ □ L

3. D □ N □

4. H □ N □ K □ □

Color them all !

Learn how to draw a reindeer! Draw and color a reindeer according to the template below across the designated boxes.

which one is different?

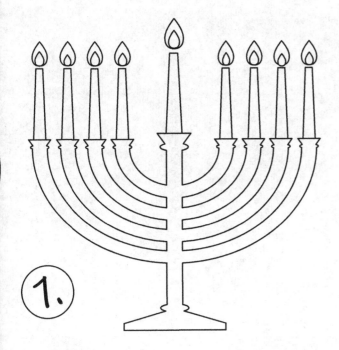

1.

2.

3.

4.

Color them all !

Find and pair with lines the same characters.

Color them all !

```
P D J E W I S H L N D M
H A O U K K A H C W T E
S E D N J B C H S I L N
T P E R U C A Q E N E O
A B C O R T A C D E H R
R C E B S R S N Z N R A
E M M U U M A A D L Y H
S C B I L D R E N I T E
A E E O N D A T P S E M
T R R J D R E I D E L S
N I G H T N R I T Y I E
W S O W I N T E R O N R
```

- dreidel   - menorah   - candies
- jewish   - donuts   - winter
- night   - december

See the solution on the next page :)

P D J E W I S H L N D M
H C O U R K Y K C W T E
P E D N J B C H S I L N
O P E R U C A Q E N E O
A B C O R T A C D E H R
L C E B S R S N Z N R A
E M M U U M A A D L Y H
S C B I L D R E N I T I
A E E O B D A T P S E M
T R R J D R E I D E L S
N I G H T N R I T Y I P
W S O W I N T E R O N R

Find and pair with lines the same characters.

Color them all !

Write the missing numbers:

2 3 5 8 10 13 16 18

Color them all !

Find 6 differences between the pictures.

Color them all !

Write the missing letters in the blank
Spaces so that they form the correct word

1. | T | | | A | |

2. | P | | | S | E | | |

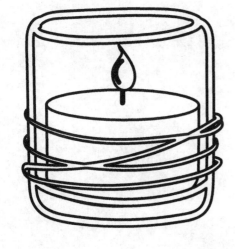

3. | C | | N | | | E |

4. | | | I | |

Color them all !

Help dreidels find their way to each other :)
Good luck!

Learn how to draw coins! Draw and color coins according to the template below across the designated boxes.

which one is different?

Color them all !

Find 8 words related to Hanukkah.
Search words in directions:

```
P D J E W I S H L C D M
K A O U K K A H C A T E
P I S T O R Y H S N L N
O P S G A M E Q E D E O
T B C L R T H C D L M R
A C E B E R O N Z E I A
T M M U U V L A D L R H
O C B I L D I E N I A E
A E E O N D D T P S C M
T R R J D R A I D E L S
N I G H T N Y I T Y E E
W Q S U F G A N I J O T
```

- Kislev
- potato
- story
- game
- holiday
- sufganijot
- candle
- miracle

See the solution on the next page :)

```
P D W F S B S H L C D M
K A O U K K A H C A T E
P I S T O R Y H S N L N
O P S G A M E Q E D E O
T B C L R T H C D L M R
A C E B E R O N Z E I A
T M M U U V L A D L R H
O C B I L D I E N I A E
A E E O N D D T P S C M
T R R J D R A I D E L S
N I G H T N Y I T Y E E
W Q S U F G A N I J O T
```

Count the items and connect them with a line to the correct answer.

6

2

5

3

Color them all !

Find 6 differences between the pictures.

Color them all !

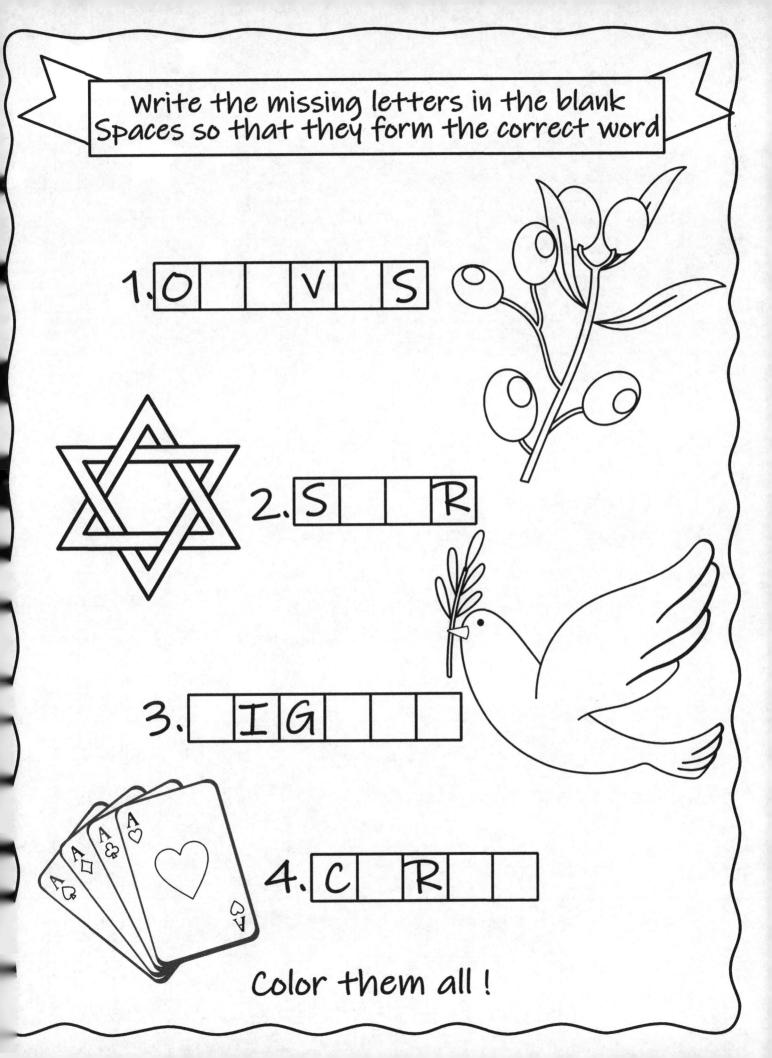

1. O | | | V | | S

2. S | | | R

3. | | I | G | | |

4. C | | R | |

Color them all !

P L A T K E S H O C D M
C H A N U K A H L A T E
P I A T O R Y H I N L N
O P S N A M E Q V D E O
T B P L U T H C E L P R
A D R B E K O N S E R A
T C A R D S K A D L E H
O Q Y I L D I I N I S E
A E E O N D D T A S E M
T R R J D R A I D H N S
N I G H L I G H T Y T E
W Q S U F G A N I J O T

- Chanukah   - prayer   - hanukkiah
- present   - latkes   - light
- olives   - cards

See the solution on the next page :)

```
P L A T K E S H O C D M
C H A N U K A H L F T E
P I A T O R Y H I T L N
D P S N A M E Q V D E O
T B P L U T H C E L P R
R D R B E K O N S I R A
T C A R D S K A D L E H
O Q Y I L D I I N I S E
U E E O N D D T A S E M
T R R J D R A I D H N S
N I G H L I G H T Y T E
W V A U J K A Y I R W T
```

Help the dove find its way to the branch :) Good luck!

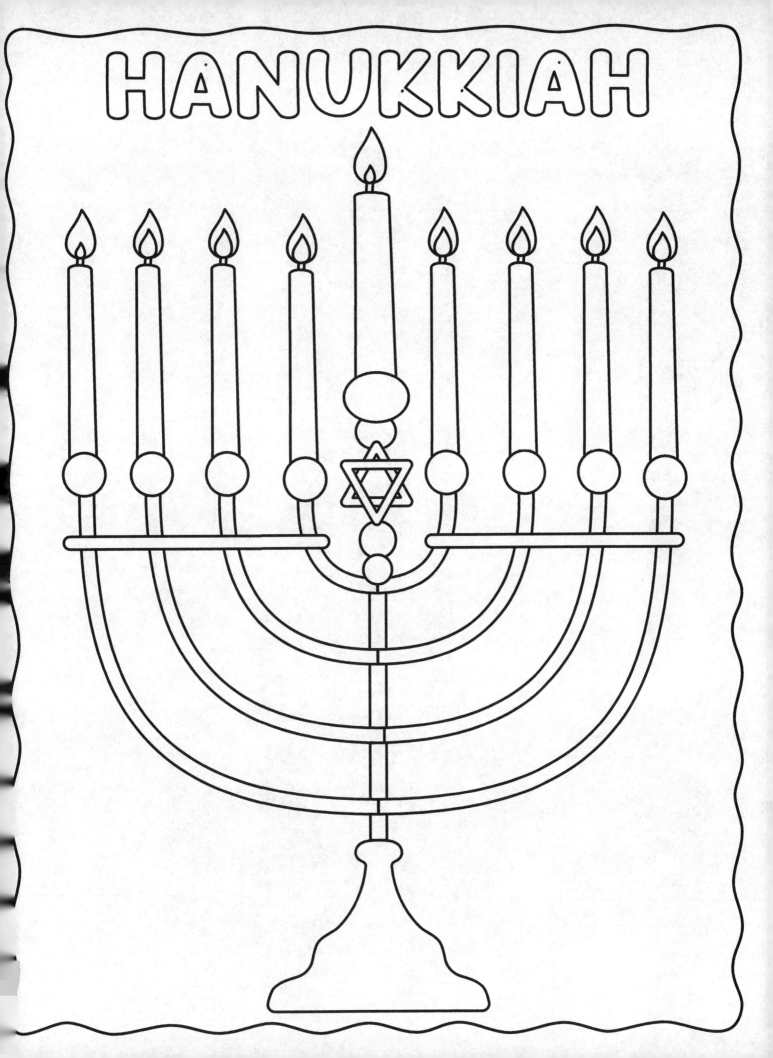

Learn how to draw a dreidel! Draw and color a dreidel according to the template below across the designated boxes.

Connect the elements with their shadows with a line.

Color them all !

Let's color the star of David !

JEWISH STAR

The Star of David !

Learn how to draw a foxy! Draw and color a foxy according to the template below across the designated boxes.

Yours notes

Yours notes

Made in the USA
Las Vegas, NV
20 December 2024